TWEETY'S GLOBAL PATROL™

By Jean Lewis
Illustrated by Joseph Messerli

A GOLDEN BOOK • NEW YORK

Western Publishing Company, Inc., Racine, Wisconsin 53404

"Global Patrol!" Tweety chirped into a phone. "That's wight. Wemember the twee R's—*we*duce, *we*use, and *we*cycle!"

He took another call. "Global Patrol! How do you wecycle junk mail? Easy. Carpet your bird cage with it!"

RINN-G.

"Global Patrol," Tweety trilled. "Are there ways to save water? Abso*wute*ly! Limit your shower to two minutes. Fill your bathtub only half full!

"But don't stop watering your plants," Tweety continued. "Use wecycled water! Keep a bucket in the kitchen, and save the rinse water from your spinach for your geraniums."

RINN-G!

"Global Patrol, Tweety here!" he trilled once more. "Stwing? Save every piece, and you'll soon have a ball of wecycled stwing the size of a bowling ball."

When the phone rang for what seemed like the hundredth time, a furious Sylvester woke up from his nap.

"Sufferin' succotash!" he exploded. "A pussycat can be pushed just so far!"

In one flying leap, Sylvester jumped from his
stool to a tall plant stand beside Tweety's cage.

"There's no livin' with this dumb bird since he
started this Global Patrol stuff!" Sylvester growled,
angrily switching his tail.

"I know. I'll recycle this bird"—he said, licking
his chops—"from pest to snack!"

"Puddy tat awert!" cried Tweety, sounding the alarm. "HEWP!" He wanted Granny to see what Sylvester was doing.

But Granny was outside and couldn't hear Tweety's alarm.

Startled by the alarm, Sylvester lurched backward and grabbed at a fern hanging over his head.

"Help!" he yelled, swinging back and forth wildly and hitting Tweety's cage like a punching bag.

"Yow-*wee*!" Sylvester screamed as the fern slipped from its hook on the ceiling.

The astonished cat hit the floor rolling—on top of Granny's giant ball of recycled string. Struggling to keep his balance, Sylvester sped toward the kitchen at top speed.

"What a good ol' puddy tat!" Tweety chirped, flying after him. "He just invented a new use for wecycled stwing!"

As he whizzed by the kitchen sink, Sylvester
grabbed the faucet to stop himself. Instead, he
turned on the cold water full-blast.

"Stop, you water waster!" cried Tweety.

For fear Granny would catch him wasting water, Sylvester turned off the faucet. But that wasn't enough for Tweety.

"Save that water!" Tweety chirped. He grabbed the sink stopper and dropped it into place.

"Look out for the window!" warned Tweety as he zoomed into the living room behind Sylvester.

Peering around the fern, Sylvester swerved just in time.

When Granny looked in the window, she wasn't sure *what* she had seen!

"Watch out for the goldfish bowl!" cried Tweety. Sylvester tried to swerve again, but it was too late. As he hit the end table, the water and the fish flew into the air.

Sylvester dropped the fern and grabbed the bowl. As he rolled around the room, he tried to catch the fish and the water.

Tweety was right beside him. "To the *left*!" he yelled. "No, over to the *right*!"

Sylvester somehow got everything back in the bowl.

"You *did* it!" cried Tweety. "You saved the glass, the water, *and* the widdle fishies!"

"Don't forget the moss," Sylvester muttered.

Next Sylvester rolled into the kitchen, scattering a bag full of empty bottles.

"Mustn't forget to wecycle those bottles!" warned Tweety.

"*And* these cans!" he chirped.

Sylvester didn't see Tweety tip over the bag of empty cans until the crazed cat rolled right into them.

"Sufferin' succotash!" Sylvester cried, clapping one paw over his eyes.

"Right this way, Puddy Tat!" said Tweety,
holding the back door wide open.

Sylvester rolled down the back steps, scattering
a pile of newspapers and landing by the trash cans.
Through the ringing in his ears he heard Granny
call, "Sylvester, where are you?"

"Ooooh, that puddy tat's in big twouble now!"
said Tweety sweetly.

"Must get this picked up before Granny comes!"
Sylvester gasped, racing back up the steps into the
kitchen. First he tossed the empty cans and bottles
back into their recycling containers.

"How about those newspapers?" Tweety called.
Sylvester hurried down the back steps to restack
the newspapers.

Back in the kitchen, Sylvester saw the stopped-up sink. That water had to be recycled! Sylvester scooped it into a bucket.

RECYCLED WATER ONLY

He mopped up the water he'd spilled and breathed a sigh of relief—until he remembered the fern.

"Granny's favorite plant!" he cried and dashed into the living room.

Sylvester quickly picked up the
fallen fern. Then he leapt to the
plant stand and reattached
the fern to its hook.

"Dear little Tweety," said Granny as she came in from the garden. "Always so busy trying to save the planet!"

Granny turned to Sylvester. "As usual, you're leaving it up to someone else!" she said, shaking her head. "Why can't *you* ever get involved?"

Sylvester groaned. "Sufferin' succotash," he said to himself. "If she only knew!"